Kung Fu Katy

and a piece of cake

with

Match of the day

Two stories by Sally-Ann Lever
Illustrated by David Pace

LONGMAN

It was early Saturday morning and Kung Fu Katy and her mum were busy preparing a very special birthday cake for Dot Wiggle, the little old lady who lived next door.

Even though there was an eighty-nine-year age gap between them, Kung Fu Katy considered Dot Wiggle to be one of her best and closest friends.

They went tree-climbing and raspberry-picking together, fishing, canoeing and conker-hunting together, roller-skating, dress-making, swimming, gyming and bike-racing together and, apart from being extremely hard of hearing, there was not an acrobatic, fun or lively thing that the little old lady couldn't do. She was simply marvellous.

"Come on, Katy – stop day-dreaming," said Mrs Peep. "We've still got loads to do. Now, you go and fetch the baking tins while I weigh out all the ingredients. This cake has got to be big enough to feed fifty starving guests."

"Oooooooh yummy! Will you make it a creamy chocolate cake, Mum?"

"CREAMY?" she replied. "CHOCOLATE?" she cried. "Katy, it'll be the smoothest, creamiest chocolate cake that's ever been baked in this world! Just remember the saying: *You'll never risk a rotten cake, if it's whipped and whisked before it's baked!"*

And she poured all the flour and sugar, eggs and butter into a big plastic bowl.

She plugged in the whisk, flicked down the switch and ...

WHAM! – BANG! – POOOOOOOOOOOFF!

... the electric wire, whisk and plug suddenly BURST into a thousand sizzling sparks, sending Mrs Peep shooting through the room in a puff of smoke and crashing right under the kitchen table.

"Oh, Mummy! Mummy! Are you all right?" yelled Kung Fu Katy, as she rushed over to poor Mrs Peep, who was lying flat on her back on the floor.

"Never mind about me," wailed Mrs Peep. "WHAT ABOUT THE CAKE? THE CAKE! Oh dear me, it'll never be rich and creamy now – it won't even be ready for the party! Oh Katy, whatever are we going to do?"

"Don't worry, Mum, you just stay right where you are and leave everything to me."

Kung Fu Katy peered at the miserable, lumpy mixture, all clotted and cloggy and clumped-up in the bowl. Slowly, she closed her eyes ... stood tall and straight ... took in two long, deep breaths, and – in one sudden swoosh – she kicked off her shoes and, as quick as two flickers, she yanked up her sleeves, stuffed her skirt in her knickers and, with ten tiny fingers packed with power, she plunged her hands deep into the eggs and flour!

BANG! BLAST! CHOP! CHOP! CHOP! – Kung Fu Katy couldn't stop.

Each finger spun, shook and trembled with the pounding power of a pumping pneumatic drill – whirrrrrrrrrrrrrrrrrrrrrmmmmmmmm! – each one exploding like ten sticks of dynamite – beating, bashing and whipping all that gooey gunge into a thick, creamy, golden sponge.

Then she poured the mixture into fourteen baking tins, ready for Mrs Peep to pop into the oven.

"Okey-dokey, Mum, it's all ready. You can come out now."

Mrs Peep crawled out from under the kitchen table, flabbergasted at the sight she saw.

"KATY! How on earth did you EVER do that?"

"Oh, it was easy," sighed Katy. "I just whisked it by hand!"

"Well, I never," gasped Mrs Peep. "It's the smoothest mixture I've ever seen. You never fail to amaze me, Katy. You really are a very clever girl."

And she popped all the tins into the oven, washed the dishes and cleaned up the kitchen floor.

One hour and ten minutes later, all the sponges were cooked and cooled. Mrs Peep and Katy stacked each one on top of the other and spent ages building a cake that stood a metre tall and proud, completely covered in cascading clouds of thick, whipped cream and rippling rolls of rich, dark chocolate.

Mrs Peep stood back to admire their spectacular creation.

"It's a masterpiece!" she beamed. "An absolute masterpiece!"

She went upstairs for a wash and tidy-up, while Kung Fu Katy settled herself comfortably in front of the telly, to watch the remainder of her favourite Saturday morning cartoons.

Suddenly, the TV went all crackly and a very serious newscaster, with thickly rimmed spectacles and a spotty bow tie, appeared on the screen.

"I'm afraid we have to interrupt this television programme with a very important newsflash. A highly dangerous and evil robber by the name of Jim Slim, The Criminal King, has escaped from Locktight Prison, in the Catchem area. He travelled up to London in a stolen car, tied up the staff at a motorway McDonald's – stealing seven hamburgers and a portion of chips – before breaking into a pet-shop to steal one of the most horrifically dangerous, venomous snakes that's ever wriggled the earth. The creature is thought to be concealed within a red box, hidden somewhere inside The Criminal King's clothing."

A picture of Jim Slim's revolting, slimy face appeared on the screen. His evil eyes beamed beneath a pair of beastly, bushy eyebrows and a blue tattoo of a king's crown lay branded across his forehead.

"PLEASE," continued the newscaster, *"do not be fooled by this man's appearance. Not only is he paper-thin – enabling his body to slip through cracks and doorways – he is also a dirty trickster and KING of all disguises."*

The newscaster leant forward and peered *very, very* seriously into the screen.

"Ladies and gentlemen, boys and girls, we believe this man to be viciously vile and wicked – and the snake is even worse. Should you come across either of the two creatures, don't talk to them, touch them or look at them – just run for your life and contact a local police station.

This is Gordon Heavens, saying PLEASE! ... be careful, behave and BEWARE! Thank you."

Kung Fu Katy stared at the TV screen as it crackled and fizzed and the cartoon reappeared and continued on its wacky way.

But she couldn't concentrate.

A cold shiver ran down the notches of her spine as she thought of that terrible man and snake roaming the streets – perhaps preparing to pounce at any time.

Katy closed her eyes for a minute, calmly allowing the image of Jim Slim, The Criminal King, to register itself firmly upon her brain.

Then she crouched onto the floor and lapsed into two hundred and fifty press-ups. She raced up the stairs, washed her face and hands and changed into a gorgeous, pink party dress that swished and billowed over six of her frilliest petticoats.

She popped a little perfume behind her ears and proudly pinned on a shiny silver medal which she had just won in a recent Kung Fu competition, beating men and women ten times her age and size.

Katy gazed at herself in the mirror and tingled with excitement. She suddenly forgot all about that terrible newsflash and couldn't wait to get to the party.

So, without wasting another second, she rushed down the stairs and into the kitchen to help Mrs Peep pack the magnificent birthday cake into a huge cardboard box.

Then they walked out of the house and down the path to join a crowd of people who had secretly gathered, whispering and giggling, outside Dot Wiggle's house, at exactly three o'clock.

Well, everyone was there. EVERYONE!

Friends and neighbours with their children and pets, each one dressed in their very best, carrying packages, plates and parcels piled up high to the sky!

"Oooooo, look!" cried Mrs Peep. "Look who's over there!"

A big, bouncy woman in a frilly, fancy, lavender dress, with a gigantic mountain of squiggly hair, was jumping up and down and waving frantically.

"Yooooo-hooooo! Yooooo-hooooo! We're over here! Over here!"

"YIPPEEEEEE!" yelled Katy. "It's Aunty Dolly. Hooray! Hooray!"

"And oh, dear me," exclaimed Mrs Peep, covering her face with her hands, "look who's up there!"

"Where?" said Katy.

"Up there – in that tree over there ..."

Kung Fu Katy looked up and saw two filthy figures dressed in matching tartan suits, all twisted and tangled and hanging upside down in the branches. They were merrily flicking squashed-up berries and other horrible things down at the crowd below.

"HIYA KATY! IT'S US – HUGHIE AND HENRY HORROR!"

"So I can see!" laughed Katy. "Hey, why don't you come down and say a proper hello?"

"Well, we started to climb up this tree," explained Henry.

"But then we got into a bit of a rut," said Hughie.

"'Cos we got stuck," said Henry.

"So we started to shout – 'cos we couldn't get out – then we got bored and fed up," said Hughie.

"So we thought we'd fling a few things down – while we were hanging around," explained Henry.

"WELL, YOU'D BETTER CLIMB DOWN RIGHT NOW!" boomed Aunty Dolly. "DO YOU HEAR ME? –

RIGHT THIS MINUTE – BEFORE I BUNG YOU ON THE NEXT TRAIN BACK TO BRIGHTON!"

"We can't, Mum, we're STUCK!" squalled Henry.

"ROOTED!" bawled Hughie.

"Don't worry," called Katy, "I'll help you. Just hang on another minute."

"Well, you'd better hurry," whispered Miss Pinkie from number 7. "Dot Wiggle might hear us and then the whole surprise will be spoilt."

"I don't think we need worry about that," sighed Mr Button from number 12. "The poor old dear can't even hear her own front door bell."

But Kung Fu Katy wasn't listening to anybody.

Carefully she crouched down onto all fours.

She lifted her head and firmly focused her eyes on to the trunk of the tree. And as everyone turned around and looked up at Hughie and Henry Horror, Katy kicked off her shoes and, as quick as two flickers, she yanked up her sleeves, stuffed her skirt in her knickers, she leapt off the ground and, with a MIGHTY big blow, soared through the sky, roaring **"YAAAAAAAAA-SOOWWWWWW!"** BANG! BLAST! CHOP! CHOP! CHOP!

Kung Fu Katy couldn't stop.

Her thrashing legs charged the air like a couple of bashing bulldozers – **Whhhhhhoooooooooooo oooooooooooooooooooooooooosssssssshhhhhhhhhh!** – and she thumped the trunk with such a magnificent kick – WHHHHHHHHHHHHHAAAAAAAMMMMMMMM! – that Hughie and Henry Horror bombed out of the tree like a pair of bullets and crashed one after the other into Dot Wiggle's front door, with the biggest bang you've ever heard in all your life.

BANG! BANG!

"Well done, boys!" praised Mr Christmas from number 44. "She's bound to have heard that! Come on everybody – quickly – let's get ready, she'll be coming any minute now!"

Hughie and Henry scuttled back to the crowd.

Everybody huddled together and watched and waited as Dot Wiggle's front door slowly, slowly, peeled open and she popped her head out from around the corner.

"SURPRISE! SURPRISE! SURPRISE!" they all yelled.

All the people clapped and cheered and sang Happy Birthday at the very tops of their voices, so that the familiar tune of that jubilant song roared through the air like a boom-town rhapsody.

Dot Wiggle's eyes filled with tears of joy.

"Well, jeepers creepers, sniff my sneakers – what a wonderful and joyous surprise!" she cried. "Fancy all my friends and neighbours coming to share my ninety-fifth birthday, without me knowing a thing. Well, come in everybody! Come on! Come in! Let's get this party on the road – Whooooooopeeeeeeee!"

Everyone piled into the little cottage and busily got to work, setting the table with their sandwiches, cakes, crisps and jellies, handing Dot Wiggle their carefully wrapped-up presents, putting on pop records and pouring out lemonade, Coca-Cola and bubbling champagne.

Soon everyone was dancing and singing and joking and giggling and having an absolutely marvellous and wonderful time.

Suddenly, there were three loud thumps at the door.

THUMP!
THUMP!
THUMP!

"I wonder who that can be?" queried Mrs Peep. "I'm sure everybody's here."

"I'll go! I'll go!" cried Dot Wiggle, delighted at the prospect of another guest.

And she opened the door to find a rather peculiar-looking lady standing on the front doorstep, dressed in a funny coat and hair-do, with the most unusual, hairy legs, stuffed into a pair of big, black trainers.

"Do I know you?" enquired Dot Wiggle politely.

"No," replied the unfamiliar figure in a deep, gruff voice. "I'm Miss Smith, the new lady that's moved in up the road. I was feeling a bit lonely and left out and I was wondering if I could come over and join in for a bit."

"Why, of course you can," replied Dot Wiggle, cupping a hand over an ear. "We've got loads of tasty food and drink, and you certainly look like you could do with fattening up a bit! So please, take your coat off and enjoy yourself."

"NO! I'd rather keep it on," snapped the lady, "because I've got something special in my pocket."

"No, no, there's no special need to lock it," replied Dot Wiggle. "We're perfectly safe around here, you know!"

"Not LOCK IT!" yelled the lady impatiently. "POCKET! I've got something special in my POCKET!"

"Very well then, suit yourself. You must feel the cold a bit, being *that* skinny! Still, please come in and feel free to help yourself to anything you want."

"Well, hee! hee! hee! Isn't THAT a coincidence?" sniggered the lady. "That's exactly what I had in mind."

"And if you want the loo," said Dot, "it's upstairs and first on the right."

Then Dot Wiggle waddled off to dance to her favourite Michael Jackson record with the rest of her friends at the party, leaving the peculiar Miss Smith to wander around the room on her own.

"Cor, she looks a bit funny," said Henry.

"Who?" said Hughie.

"That woman who looks like her hair's stuck on back to front!" chuckled Henry.

Hughie turned to look at the lady and instantly crumpled to the floor in a fit of snorting giggles. "Hee! hee! hee! oooooh! ha! ha! ha!"

But Katy never flinched an inch.

Her whole body froze solid to the spot.

Every hair and muscle stood to attention as her eyes narrowed into two thin, squinting slits, and stared piercingly into the woman's face.

What was it?

What was it that seemed so strange and familiar about that odd-looking woman?

Was it the ill-fitting coat with its tight, cropped sleeves that stopped short at the elbow...? No. Probably not.

Was it those grubby hands with their long, filthy, fiddly fingers ...? Doubtful.

Or was it the way that scrawny body edged its way around the room, discreetly brushing all the little trinkets and treasures along its way ...? No. No way.

It was the eyes!

Those unmistakable beady, black eyes, shining through a fringe of wonky hair, INSTANTLY triggered that morning's newsflash onto Katy's calmly conditioned Kung Fu memory and mind.

Katy's eyelids flickered, as her eyes penetrated deeper into the woman's face and, without a question of a doubt, she knew.

She knew that the most despicably dangerous and wanted man in Britain was standing in that very room, veiled beneath that conspicuous and curious disguise.

Oblivious to all her surroundings, Katy's unflinching gaze continued to follow the villain around the room. She watched, very carefully, as his hand patted the pocket in his coat. And he smiled, a thin, vile, thievish smile, before he disappeared out through the door and into the kitchen.

"Well, well, well," he snarled. "Just look what we've got in here! A great big, monster birthday cake! Ah-ha, just the perfect place for my delicious little plan. After all, what trick could be dirtier or more divine than one devised by meeeeeeeeee – THE KING OF CRIME! **YEEEEEEEE-HA-HA-HA-HA-HARRRrrrrrr!"**

The devious Jim Slim plunged his hand into his pocket and pulled out a red box. Slowly, he lifted the lid, revealing the fat body of a coiled-up snake that lay silently squirming and wriggling around inside.

Jim Slim's mouth curled into a mean, devilish smile. **"YEEEEEEEEE-HAARRRRRRRR!"** he roared.

"Now do your job, my little snake,
and go plant your poison inside this cake,
and when they're writhing with tummy ache,
I'll slip through the window to make my ESCAPE!
YEEEEEE-HA-HA-HA-HA-HARRRRR!"

The snake lifted its head and sniffed. Within one split second, its slithery body shot out of the box and dived straight into the cake, where it frenziedly spat and squirted its venomous poison throughout the whole of that creamy sponge.

Jim Slim was thrilled that his party trick had gone so well. He licked his lips and rubbed his hands and, with a short, sharp glance over both his shoulders, he secretly slid up the stairs and slipped into Dot Wiggle's bedroom, where he closed the door firmly behind him.

Well, Jim Slim's eyes lit up like electric light bulbs when he saw what lay in front of them. He hadn't been for a good old steal for ages and he could hardly wait to start.

"Ooooh, goodie, goodie," he greedily sniggered. "What a LOVELY lot of loot in here! Now let's see, where shall I begin? Oooh yes, a nice silver frame ... ooooooh lovely, I'll have that ... Ahhhhhh, a pretty ruby brooch ... oh definitely ... I could do with that.

"Mmmmmm, a shiny gold hat pin ... oh yes, I really fancy that ... and this ... and them ... and all of that ... those chains, trinkets and pearly things, her necklace, bracelets and all her rings, that watch, that clock, that silver plate, that bottle of sherry – those After Eights, and this and that and all of those – her socks and shoes and all her clothes, her dolly and trolley and pom-pom hat, these and those and all of that. Pyjamas – pillows – blankets – sheets – her sweets – treats – and midnight feasts, and oooooooh and ahhhhhhh and eeeeeeee and ummmmmmm and yum-yum, yum-yum, yum-yum, YUM!"

He scooped and scraped up all the contents of her dressing-table and drawers and stuffed EVERYTHING into a huge, black sack that had been crumpled-up in his pocket.

Then he tiptoed out of the door and crept into the next bedroom where his mouth dripped and dribbled in excitement, as he spotted all the coats and bags and presents sprawled across the floor.

Jim Slim's fingers instantly delved into every pocket, purse and bag, grabbing and snatching all the money and private possessions, before ripping open the presents and stashing them ALL away inside the sack.

"Corrrrrrr, what a smashing time I've had at this party!" he gloated. "And now's the perfect time to make my flying getaway. **YEEEEEEEEE-HA-HA-HA-HA-HARRRRRRRR!"**

As quick as a flash, he opened the window, lowered the sack onto the ground and climbed up onto the ledge.

SUDDENLY, there was a terrific CRASH! **Shhhhhhhhhhhhhhhhhhhheeeeeeeeeeerrrrrrrrrr – BANG!**

Kung Fu Katy BURST out through the cupboard door and, with one almighty thunderous R O A R, she leapt onto his back and CRASHED him to the floor. **"KEEEEEEEEEEE-YOWWWWWWWWWW! –** NOT SO FAST YOU FILTHY FIEND! I KNOW EXACTLY WHO YOU ARE!"

Spitting and cursing, Jim Slim tried to wriggle from beneath her monster clutches, but it was no use. Kung Fu Katy's strength was so staggering that she had him fixed to the floor like a magnet.

"GET OFF ME!" he roared. "GET OFF ME! GET OFF ME! GET OFF MEEEE!"

At that very second, Mrs Peep and all the party guests stormed in through the bedroom door.

"KATY! YOU NAUGHTY GIRL! WHAT IN HEAVEN'S NAME DO YOU THINK YOU'RE DOING? Fancy trying to spoil Dot Wiggle's party by practising your martial arts on one of her poor, innocent guests. Really, Katy! I'm absolutely appalled. This time you have gone TOO FAR!"

"But Mum! Mum! This ISN'T a lady – it's Jim Slim, The Criminal King, the most wanted man in Britain! I saw him on the telly this morning. He's the most dangerous robber that's ever escaped from prison! He's in a disguise and that's a WIG on his head! You'll see – there's a tattoo on his forehead! And he's planted a snake in Dotty's cake that's going to poison EVERYONE any minute NOW! It's TRUE! I SWEAR IT! I saw him do it with my very own eyes!"

"Don't be so RIDICULOUS!" yelled Mrs Peep. "Snakes, robbers, whatever next? You've been watching too much television, young lady – that's what your trouble is. Now, let go of poor Miss Smith this instant and PULL YOURSELF TOGETHER!"

Poor Katy.

For once in her life she was speechless.

She let go of Jim Slim, as all the guests shook their heads from side to side and tutted in utter disgust. Jim Slim stood up and straightened his coat and hair.

"Well ... erm ... I think I'll be off then," he stammered.

"Thanks for the party and see you another day. Goodbye!"

"Oh, don't be daft – we wouldn't hear of it," insisted Mrs Peep. "You're not going anywhere until you've completely recovered and had a nice cup of tea and a big slice of that delicious cake."

"Cake!" exclaimed Jim Slim. "CAKE? Oh no, I can't eat cake. I'm ALLERGIC to cake! It gives me terrible wind."

"No need to worry about a silly thing like that," said Mrs Peep comfortingly. "It happens to the best of us."

And before Jim Slim had a chance to say another word, all the people gathered around him and led him down the stairs.

They brushed up his coat and smoothed down his hair.

They hugged, patted and stroked him.

They rushed and fussed around him.

And they brought him a huge plate of sandwiches, sausage rolls, sweets, chocolate, jelly and ice cream and a hot cup of tea with two sugars and a dash of milk.

"I just can't tell you how sorry we are," said Mr Toff from number 8. "This is such a friendly neighbourhood and nothing like this has ever happened before. I just can't imagine what came over our Katy. She's normally such a sweet little girl."

"Oh well, let's forget all about that now," said Aunty Dolly brightly, "and bring in that scrumptious cake."

Everybody smiled and nodded in agreement as Jim Slim shot out of his chair like a bolt.

"Oh no! Don't do that!" he exclaimed. "Please, please, it really isn't necessary."

"Now you just stay right where you are, Miss Smith," said Aunty Dolly, pushing him back in his seat. "After all that rumpus upstairs, you deserve the BIGGEST slice of all!"

She disappeared into the kitchen, lit the candles, and returned carrying the mouth-watering creation that flamed and flickered with ninety-five candles and lit up the room like a thousand stars.

Everyone "Oooooh'd" and "Ahhhh'd" and licked their lips as Dot Wiggle blew out the candles and raised the knife to cut the cake.

"STOP, DOTTY! STOP! Don't cut it – not before you've made a speech!"

"Very well, then. Short speeches are best: thank you all for this wonderful party. Now stand back, kids – for here's the REAL surprise!"

Silence fell.

Fifty faces gulped in shock and horror as little Dot Wiggle leapt out of her chair, flew through the air and in one startling swoosh – she kicked off her shoes and, as quick as two flickers, she yanked up her sleeves, stuffed her skirt in her knickers, and, with bulging biceps once trained for fighting, she CHARGED through the air like a flash of lightning!

BANG! BLAST! CHOP! CHOP! CHOP!

Old Dot Wiggle just could not stop.

She smashed her fists through the centre of the cake with such monstrous force that it exploded into a spewing volcano of gushing slush, sploshing the guests with lashings of cream and plastering the snake SMACK – BANG against the wall, in a cage of cemented sponge. **WHOOOOOOOOOOOOOO OOOOOOOOOOOOSHHHH – S P L A T!**

Well, nobody could believe their eyes.

Everybody gasped and fell to the floor in fright.

A long, thin, pink tongue could be seen flickering in a tiny hole in the sponge, as the bogus Miss Smith dived off her chair and charged like a bull towards the door.

"QUICK!" cried Katy. "LATCH HIM! SNATCH HIM! GRAB HIM! CATCH HIM!"

Within one sensational second, every single person at the party charged forward and jumped on top of the struggling Jim Slim.

Kung Fu Katy ripped off one of her petticoats, wrenched him from under the pile and tied him securely to a chair. Then she snatched the wig off his head, revealing the tattooed crown of evidence stamped across his forehead.

"There you are! Look!" she puffed. "You see, I WAS telling the truth!"

Panting with exhaustion, Mrs Peep ran off to call the police while everyone crowded around Katy and clapped and cheered and patted her on the back.

"Three cheers for Katy – Hip Hip Hooray! Hip Hip Hooray! Hip Hip HOOOOOOOORAY!"

"I knew my best friend Katy would never lie," sniffed Dot Wiggle. "And besides, I saw that very same newsflash myself this morning."

"Thanks, Dotty," said Kung Fu Katy. "I knew I could rely on you."

Twenty-three seconds later, a band of sixty policemen came screeching down the path and marched into the house, thrashing their fists and truncheons frantically through the air.

"WHERE IS HE?" they roared. "**WHERE IS HE?**"

"Over here," said Kung Fu Katy quietly. "All tied up and ready to go."

"Well, bless my soul!" gasped the Chief Inspector, gawping at the snivelling Jim Slim, all crumpled and rumpled and tied to the chair.

"How you EVER managed to recognise and collar and capture the most desperately hunted villain in Britain is something I shall never, never know!"

"Oh, it was nothing," said Kung Fu Katy, smiling sweetly. "It was a piece of cake!"

Kung Fu Katy's

Match of the day

It was a Friday lunchtime, and Kung Fu Katy and her friends were sitting in class, reeling and bursting with excitement. Their form teacher, Miss Mellow, was getting married the following day to Mr Windham, the music teacher. She'd asked every single girl and boy in her class to be bridesmaids and page boys, and had invited all their parents and all the teachers too.

Miss Mellow was so grateful to Father Godfrey for allowing all these people to attend the wedding service that she'd arranged for a special charity football match to take place that very afternoon. The money raised would pay for the village church roof repairs. And the children could hardly wait.

"Let's have a little hush now!" said Miss Mellow, clapping her hands together. "I know you're terribly excited, but The Wexley Whoppers will be here at any minute. So, I'd like the boys to run off and get changed into their football kits, and the girls to collect twenty pence from each spectator, before seating them around the pitch. Katy Peep, I'd like you to come with me please, to welcome the opposition down at the school gate. Right. Now is everybody clear about what they have to do?"

"YES, MISS MELLOW!"

"Off you go, then. And boys, the best of luck!"

The boys hurried off to the locker rooms.

The girls scurried off to find paper, pens and empty pots for the money, while Kung Fu Katy and Miss Mellow walked along the path and down to the gate to greet The Wexley Whoppers.

Moments later, a big, gold coach drew up outside the school. The doors *hisssssssed* open, and a man in a diamond-studded track suit, with five bronze medallions draped around his neck and chest, breezed down the steps and hopped onto the pavement.

"Hi there, dolls! My name's Jones. Tom Jones. No relation to the star of course, but the girls think I'm just as handsome, HA-HA-HA! Now, I'm the sports master of Wexley Junior High," he continued, "and I'm proud to introduce the finest bunch of football players that you're ever likely to meet. In fact, ladies, we've NEVER lost a game yet. And, thanks to our excellent goalie Bruno Brown, no team has EVER scored against us ... BOYS! COME OUT AND SAY HELLO TO THE LADIES!"

There was a noisy shuffle, and a rowdy scuffle.

Two seconds later, a bunch of great, big, beefy, burly boys BURST out through the coach doors, spitting and shouting the most unprintable words. They pushed and shoved and scrambled into a disorderly file, yelling and chanting:

"WE'RE THE ROTTERS! THE SHOCKERS!

THE WEXLEY WHOPPERS!
SO DON'T STAND STILL – 'COS WE'RE
OUT TO KILL
AND *YOU* CAN'T JOLLY WELL STOP US!"

"That's the spirit, boys!" chuffed Mr Jones. "That's the stuff I like to hear!"

"Well, how do you do, Whoppers," said Miss Mellow politely. "Welcome to Peach Hill Primary. I must say you're a little bigger than we'd expected, but it won't matter. This is a friendly match, in aid of charity, so may the best team win!"

"Friendly?" said one of the boys. "What's that mean, sir?"

"It means that you say sorry after you've kicked somebody," replied Mr Jones.

"Charity?" said another. "What's that mean, sir?"

"Charity is when you raise money for a worthwhile cause, like Miss Mellow is doing for her local church roof. And since there's no way we're going to lose this soppy, little match, I propose to donate five pence for every goal The Whoppers score, and ten pounds for every goal Peach Hill will *never* score. Now, how does that sound?"

"Oh, that's very kind, Mr Jones," said Miss Mellow gratefully. "Thank you very much. Now, if you'd like to follow Katy and me, we'll make our way over to the pitch."

"Come on then, lads!" cried Mr Jones. "Let's follow the ladies. And remember ... we're here to BEAT 'EM, BASH 'EM, MINCE-MEAT AND THRASH 'EM, so don't give in, till you've had your win and you've crushed, mashed, squashed and flattened 'em!"

As soon as the players arrived on the pitch, the whole of Peach Hill Primary were clapping and cheering and waving their scarves and banners wildly through the air.

"COME ON, BOYS!"

"YOU CAN DO IT!"

"UP THE PEACHES!"

But Kung Fu Katy stood silently watching and

waiting. Not only were The Whoppers a bunch of great, big, blabber-mouthed bullies, but they were also twice the size of any of The Peaches and she feared for the safety of her friends.

The ref blew his whistle.

The Whoppers' centre-forward took the ball.

He charged down the pitch, shoved five Peach Hill players out of his way, and whacked the ball over the top of the goalie's head – straight into the back of the net – WHAM!

"**HOOOOOOOOOOOOORAY!**" roared The Wexley Whoppers.

"**BOOOOOOOOOOOOOOOOOOOO!**" wailed Peach Hill Primary.

"**WHOOOOOOOOOOOOOOOPEEEEEEEEEEEEE!**" chuckled Tom Jones. "That's one nil to us and five pence towards your silly church roof! Come on, lads, let's have less of the howling and more of that fouling!"

Once again, the ref blew his whistle.

The Whoppers' winger stole the ball.

He pushed, bashed and banged his way down the pitch, wounding five Peaches and making another four cry, before sloshing the ball through their legs and into the back of the goal – WHOOOOOOOOSH!

And no matter how hard they tried, it was absolutely impossible for poor Peach Hill to score a goal. At the blast of the half-time whistle, they were losing seven nil, with nine injured – including all their substitutes.

"**HOOOOOOOOOOOOOOOOOOOOOORAY!**" cried The Whoppers.

"**BOOOOOOOOOOOOOOOOOOOOOOOOOOOO!**" replied the Peach Hill spectators.

"Oh no," sighed Miss Mellow. "Those poor darlings. We've still another half to go, without any extra players or a plaster left in the box. Whatever are we going to do now?"

Kung Fu Katy's brain snapped to attention.

"Miss Mellow, let ME go on! I KNOW I could do something to help."

"Oh Katy, sweetheart," sighed Miss Mellow. "Football is no game for a girl and, besides, those boys are far too rough and dangerous. No, I'm sorry. It's simply out of the question – I definitely cannot allow it."

"PLEASE Miss Mellow – PLEEEEEEEEEASE!" begged Katy. "Just give me a chance! You MUST!"

"Come on," mocked a Whopper, "we could do with a laugh!"

Kung Fu Katy slowly looked up and crunched the bones in her knuckles.

She closed her eyes, sucked in a huge deep breath, and, with the rage of a flying torpedo, she kicked off her shoes and, as quick as two flickers, she yanked up her sleeves, stuffed her skirt in her knickers, and, with an amazing SURGE of football skill in her, she bombed round that pitch like Gary Lineker.

BANG! BLAST! CHOP! CHOP! CHOP!

Kung Fu Katy couldn't stop.

Each time the ref blew his whistle, right up until the end of the game, Katy took charge of the ball and ...

bombed it

lobbed it

headed it

volleyed it

flipped it
chipped it
chested it
dribbled it
thighed it
wiggled it
whacked it
lodged it
hammered it

rammed it down the pitch and *slammed* it firmly into the back of the goal, resulting in a final spectacular score of: Peach Hill Primary 112 – 7 The Wexley Whoppers.

Well, they couldn't believe their eyes. The crowd rocked and roared with delight and surprise. And The Wexley Whoppers were so shocked and dazed that they buried their heads in their hands and spat and cursed and yelled and cried.

For not once, in their WHOLE football career, had they ever lost a game. And there they were, devastated, crushed and defeated in one afternoon – BY A GIRL!

Kung Fu Katy walked over to Tom Jones and smiled.

"That makes a very generous donation of one thousand, one hundred and twenty pounds and thirty-five pence. I'm afraid we don't accept credit cards, but a cheque or cash will do nicely."

Mr Jones moaned and mumbled under his breath. He fumbled into his pocket and pulled out a wad of crispy notes and stuffed them furiously into Katy's hand.

"That's six months' wages, that is!" he snapped.

And he turned on his heels and stormed off back to the coach.

The Wexley Whoppers trailed miserably behind, except for Bruno Brown, the goalie.

"Don't think you can get away with making a fool out of me like that," he hissed, "because I'll be back ... MUCH SOONER THAN YOU THINK!"

Early the next morning, Kung Fu Katy rose and stretched to the sun streaming in through her bedroom window. The birds were singing, the church bells were ringing, and the sky was a perfect blue.

Mrs Peep breezed into Katy's bedroom, carrying a tray of cereal, toast and tea.

"A special treat for the Bridesmaid!" she beamed.

And she left the tray on Katy's bed, while she popped off to dress for the wedding.

But Kung Fu Katy couldn't eat a thing. She felt dizzy with excitement at the thought of the day. So she jumped out of bed and leapt into fifteen short, sharp Kung Fu kicking exercises, before slipping into the beautiful, apricot bridesmaid's dress that Miss Mellow had designed and stitched by hand for every girl in the class.

And, as a special treat for Katy, Miss Mellow had sewn not five, not ten, but fifteen of the frilliest petticoats to the underside of the skirt. It was by far

the prettiest dress that Katy had ever owned.

Then she unwrapped the head-dress from its tissue paper, and carefully pinned the ring of rosebuds and lillies onto the top of her head. For the finishing touch, she stepped into a pair of ballet shoes and placed a row of shiny beads around her neck.

Mrs Peep popped her head around Kung Fu Katy's door and smiled with pride at the sight of her daughter.

"Ooooooooooh Katy, you look absolutely beeeeeeeeeeautiful! Now, promise not to spoil that gorgeous dress. If you start any of that unladylike Kung-phooey stuff, I shall be very cross indeed."

"Don't worry, Mum," said Kung Fu Katy. "Nothing in the world could possibly happen to wreck this dress or ruin the day."

They walked out of the house, jumped into the car, and zoomed around to Miss Mellow.

All Kung Fu Katy's friends were sitting and waiting in a magnificent horse-drawn cart, which was parked outside Miss Mellow's house. The girls were in their apricot dresses, the boys in their navy blue suits.

"Hi, Katy!" called Lucy Short. "Come up here and sit next to me."

"But where's Miss Mellow?" asked Katy.

"Don't know. She hasn't come out yet."

"Maybe she's still eating breakfast," said Johnny Beer.

"Or perhaps she's in the bath!"

"Or locked in the loo!"

"Or marking our homework."

"Or fallen down the stairs."

"Or crying."

"Crying? Why should she be crying?"

"All brides cry," said Debs Lasky.

"Well, I reckon she's forgotten."

"And gone shopping."

"Or watching Tom and Jerry."

"Or gone off Mr Windham."

"Or ..."

Suddenly, everyone stopped.

A cloud of dazzling white lace appeared at the door and came floating down the path. It was Miss Mellow, looking absolutely stunning in her flowing dress and train, with the most incredible five-metre billowing veil that whirled and swirled from a crown of sparkly diamonds encircling her pretty head.

"OOOOOOOOOOOOOOOOOOOOOOOOOOOOOO OHHHHHHHHH Miss Mellow!" chimed the children.

They were so busy rushing and fussing and helping her onto the cart that nobody noticed Bruno Brown, The Whoppers' goalie, jump out of the bushes and hurl a massive pot of pepper into the horse's bucket of hay.

Bruno hadn't recovered from yesterday's thrashing, and there he was, full of hate and fury, out to seek his revenge.

"HUH! That'll teach those creepy Peaches a lesson," he snarled. "After all, NOBODY gets the better of Bruno Brown, the roughest, toughest bully in town!"

He staggered off down the road, in an uncontrollable fit of giggles.

Miss Mellow sat down.

The driver took the reins.

And the horse stopped munching ... he shuffled and shivered ... he buckled and quivered ... AND OH MY WORD! In one horrendous, devastating flash, that huge, white stallion took off down the road like a wild, frantic beast, charging in and out of screeching cars, through trees, brooks and bushes, over lorries, buses, bikes and benches, tearing past Bruno Brown, snatching his trouser leg and hurling him onto the back of the cart – Whooooooooooooooooosh – PLOP!

The children were screaming.

Miss Mellow was fainting.

And the wheels of the cart were rocking and shaking.

The driver plummeted to the ground, while the horse thundered and thrashed through fields, gates, gardens and parks, the pub – the pool – and Marks and Sparks – over the bridge, under the arch – down winding lanes – down crooked paths.

Kung Fu Katy leapt to her feet.

"GET DOWN, EVERYONE – GET DOWN!"

And as they crashed to the floor of the cart, Kung Fu Katy kicked off her shoes and as quick as two flickers, she yanked up her sleeves, stuffed her skirt in

her knickers, and, with the power of a panther and the speed of a plane, she LEAPT on the horse and grabbed hold of his mane.

BANG! BLAST! CHOP! CHOP! CHOP!

Kung Fu Katy couldn't stop.

She yanked the flying reins – "**KEEEEEEEEEEEEE EEEEEEEEEEYOWWWWWWW!**" she heaved them towards her chest, and HAULED AND PULLED with all her might, "WHOAAAAAAAA BOY! WHOAAAAAAAA BOY! WHOAAAAAAAA!"

And would you believe it? Like an absolute miracle, the horse's galloping hooves screeched to a grinding halt.

"CHHAWWWW!" It fell into a gentle trot, "Clip-clop, clip-clop, clip-clop, clip ..." and arrived at the church three minutes ahead of time.

Phew!

The children and Miss Mellow jumped off the cart, still shaking and shivering with shock ... except Bruno Brown.

He was amazed at Katy's strength, dazed at her courage and OUTRAGED that she'd beaten him once again.

"BRUNO! WHAT ARE YOU DOING HERE?" yelled Kung Fu Katy.

"Just thought I'd fly by, to make sure Miss Marsh-Mellow got to the church on time," he scoffed.

Kung Fu Katy's nostrils quivered.

Bruno Brown backed away.

"Is this boy bothering you?" asked Father Godfrey.

"You can say that again," puffed Katy. "He's trying to spoil Miss Mellow's wedding."

"We'll see about that," said Father Godfrey. "Katy, take him into the church and sit him in a nice, quiet corner, away from any trouble. Then we'll deal with him after the service."

"Okey dokey, Father."

"Oh, and Katy."

"Yes, Father?"

"Make sure that, whatever happens, he doesn't touch the ropes."

Kung Fu Katy stood up on her tiptoes and grabbed Bruno by his tie. She hauled him into the church and plonked him in a chair, in a cold, far-away corner.

"Now, you just stay right there," she warned. "And remember what Father Godfrey said – whatever happens, don't you DARE touch those ropes."

"What ropes?"

"These ropes."

"Which ropes?"

"THE BELL ROPES!"

And she dashed to the back of the church, to join the parade of page boys and bridesmaids who were following Miss Mellow walking up the aisle.

Well, the organ played, and the choir sang "Here Comes the Bride." The congregation smiled and sniffed and dried their eyes. The mums and dads were clicking their cameras and waving. The teachers were clapping and "hip-hip-hooraying" – and you'll never guess who was standing right next to Mrs Peep in the third row from the front ... AUNTY DOLLY AND HUGHIE AND HENRY HORROR!

They'd come all the way up from Brighton especially to see Kung Fu Katy being a bridesmaid. And there they were, yelling and cheering and throwing huge great handfuls of confetti and rice all over the church.

"Yoooooooooooooooo-hooooooooooooooooo, Katy!" called Aunty Dolly. "Blow us a kiss!"

"Wotcher, Katy!" yelled Hughie. "Blow us a raspberry!"

"OY, KATY!" yelled Henry. "I CAN SEE YOUR KNICKERS!"

"SHHHHHHHHHHHHHHHHHHHHHHHHHHH ...!" hushed the crowd.

"They're starting ..."

Miss Mellow stood before the altar, Mr Windham at her side. Father Godfrey lifted his prayer book, and the service began.

"Ladies and gentlemen, we are gathered here today, to join these two people in holy matrimony."

"Ahhhhhhhhhhhhhhhhhhh," sighed the crowd.

"BORRRRING!" cried Bruno Brown.

"SSSSSSSSSSSSSHHHHHHHHHHHHHH!" hushed Aunty Dolly.

"Now, do you Roy Windham take Trixie Mellow to be your lawful, wedded wife, to love, honour and protect until the day you die?"

"I do," replied Mr Windham.

"I bet he does," yawned Bruno, "'cos there's nothing else to do around here."

And he gazed aimlessly around the church, until his eyes stopped, blinked, and rested on the three dangling ropes.

"I know," he sniggered, "perhaps a little light music would liven things up a bit!"

Quickly and quietly, he inched his way over to the ropes and tugged at the first droopy cord.

"DING!" went the bell.

He raised his arms and pulled the second.

"DONG!" went the bell.

He stepped over to the third and WRENCHED and PULLED and HEEEEEEEEEAVED with all his strength and might – YANK!

Suddenly, there were three earth-shattering clangs.

CLANG!

CLANG!

C L A N G !

Bruno Brown's huge, hefty body shot up the rope, pitched through the air and disappeared booming and clashing through a whopping great crack in the roof!

"HELP! HELP!" he screamed. "PLEASE SOMEBODY HELP ME! I'm stuck up in this dark, dingy hole and there's a great big nest of swarming bees up here and – OWWW! – one's just stung my

bum! Oh, SAVE ME PLEASE! SOMEBODY SAVE ME ... OUCH ... oooo ... YIKES! **HEEEEEEELPPP!**"

There fell a silenced hush ...

Little pieces of sawdust peeled away from the beams and quietly floated down.

Tiny particles of grit and grime drifted like snowflakes, and gently rested on top of the people's hats and heads.

There was an eerie creeeeeeeak ... a tiny squeak ...a grumble – a TUMBLE – A THUNDEROUS RUMBLE – and eeeeeeeeeeeeeeeee ... OOWWWW! The arched timbers of the roof began to shatter, splinter, BANG, CRACK and TWANG!

All the wedding guests pushed and shoved towards the door, fleeing from the pelting rubble and swarm of buzzing bees. Without a single moment's hesitation, Kung Fu Katy kicked off her shoes and, as quick as two flickers, she yanked up her sleeves, stuffed her skirt in her knickers, and, with a glance to check that no one was hurt, she ran round the bridesmaids and RIPPED OFF THEIR SKIRTS!

BANG! BLAST! CHOP! CHOP! CHOP! Kung Fu Katy couldn't stop.

She twisted and tied each skirt together, forming a long silken ladder, which she hurled through the air and latched onto a dangling beam.

She leapt up the knotted rungs,
grabbed the bawling Bruno Brown,
and lowered him onto the ground to safety.
But time was running out ...
The roof was caving in second by second.
The rafters were snapping,
the pulpit collapsing,
but Katy kept cool, calm and alert.

With the speed of a flying tornado, she ran up to Miss Mellow, and "KEEEEEEEEEEEEEEEEEEE EEEEEEEEEE-YOWWWWWWWWWWWWWWWW!" ripped the train off her dress, whipped the veil off her head and fastened the two together.

She thrust the huge, billowing sheet through the air, tied the edges to the top of four benches and dashed back to the crowd who were crouching down by the door.

The congregation stared up at the ceiling and GASPED in shock and terror.

The final rafter snapped. The roof caved wide open. And a shuddering storm of rock and rubble came TEARING and CRASHING down into the huge safety-net of lace, the web of delicate mesh capturing each bible and holy treasure, whilst protecting the people from a blizzard of brick, sand and stone.

Kung Fu Katy looked around the church, and for the first time in her whole life, she burst into a flood of tears.

Everything and everybody looked **ABSOLUTELY AWFUL**.

The guests, the bridesmaids, the page boys were bedraggled and filthy.

The church was a wreck.

And the bride's beautiful dress was completely ripped to shreds. Her hair was tangled. Her head-dress all mangled. And her face caked and covered in soot.

"Oh, Miss Mellow!" sobbed Katy. "Look – look what I've done to your dress! Oh, I'm so-so-sorry – how could you ever possibly forgive me?"

"Katy, darling, please don't cry," said Miss Mellow kindly.

"Thanks to you, every church treasure has been saved. Not a soul was injured or hurt. And there's enough money from the football match to pay for all the damage and repairs. Katy, you are an extremely clever and courageous little girl. I am very, very proud of you!"

The congregation flocked around Katy and hugged and squeezed and patted her.

"Well done, Katy! BRAVO!"

"Brilliant!"

"Wicked!"

"Excellent!"

Kung Fu Katy wiped away her tears.

Mr Windham took his bride into his arms and kissed her lips.

And Father Godfrey pronounced them husband and wife.